Orang

Written by Jack Gabolinscy

Orangutans are big apes.
They live in the forest.

Key

where orangutans live

Orangutans are very good
at climbing trees.
They can stay up
in the trees all day.

3

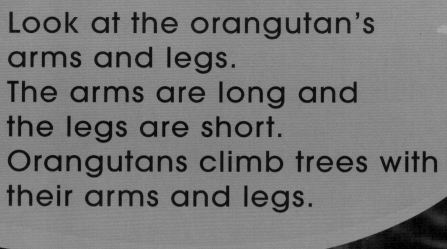

Look at the orangutan's
arms and legs.
The arms are long and
the legs are short.
Orangutans climb trees with
their arms and legs.

long arms

short legs

Orangutans don't have a tail.

Orangutans eat food in the forest.

They can eat:

 fruit and flowers

 leaves,

 insects.

leaves

baby orangutan

The orangutan mother takes care of her baby. She feeds her baby when it is hungry.

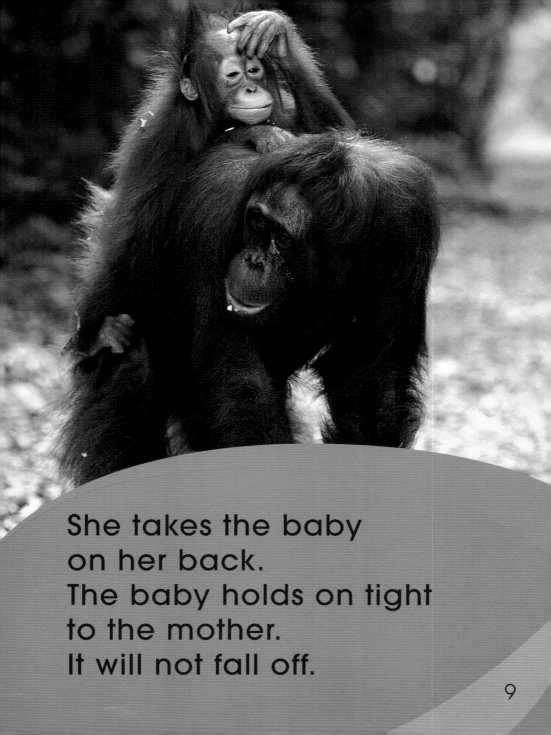

She takes the baby
on her back.
The baby holds on tight
to the mother.
It will not fall off.

9

Orangutans are very clever.
When it is raining,
the orangutan gets
a big leaf.
It goes under the leaf.
The leaf is like
an umbrella.

Orangutans make their nests up in the trees. They make their nests out of sticks and leaves. The nest will keep them safe and warm.

sticks

leaves

People go into the forests, too. They cut down all the trees. Where will the orangutans live if there are no trees?

Index

Guide Notes

Title: Orangutans
Stage: Early (3) – Blue

Genre: Nonfiction
Approach: Guided Reading
Processes: Thinking Critically, Exploring Language, Processing Information
Written and Visual Focus: Photographs (static images), Index, Labels, Map
Word Count: 177

THINKING CRITICALLY
(sample questions)
- Look at the front cover and the title. Ask the children what they know about orangutans.
- Look at the title and read it to the children.
- Focus the children's attention on the index. Ask: "What are you going to find out about in this book?"
- Ask the children what they know about the food orangutans like to eat.
- If you want to find out about the food orangutans eat, what page would you look on?
- If you want to find out where an orangutan makes a nest, what page would you look on?
- Look at page 14. Why do you think cutting down trees could be bad for the orangutans?
- Which countries do you think orangutans could live in? Why?

EXPLORING LANGUAGE

Terminology
Title, cover, photographs, author, photographers

Vocabulary
Interest words: orangutan, apes, forest, insects, umbrella
High-frequency words: very, don't, them, takes, off, there
Positional words: in, up, under, on, down, off

Print Conventions
Capital letter for sentence beginnings, periods, commas, question mark, colon